Happy Horse

For John D.

Other titles in this series include:

Daft Dog
Greedy Goat
Crazy Cow
Rude Rabbit
Bad Bear

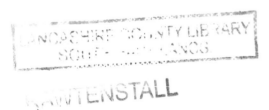
First published in hardback in Great Britain by HarperCollins Publishers Ltd in 2001
1 3 5 7 9 10 8 6 4 2
ISBN: 0-00-198353-9

Printed in Singapore by Imago

Happy Horse

Colin and Jacqui Hawkins

Collins

An imprint of HarperCollinsPublishers

085392318

This is Happy Horse.

Everyone liked Happy Horse as he was always so cheerful with a big happy grin.

"I'm a happy chappy," laughed Happy Horse as he galloped around town.

Happy Horse was very proud of his beautiful teeth. He brushed them every day until they gleamed. "What lovely laughing gear I've got," said Happy Horse as he looked in the mirror.

"I like to keep fit,"
said Happy Horse.
So every day he swam
and ran, and then
trotted off to the gym.

"A healthy horse
is a happy horse,"
said Happy Horse as
he did his exercises.

But best of all Happy Horse loved dancing
and every Saturday night he went to the
Clip Clop Club.

"I'm a hip, hop horse," laughed Happy Horse as
he whirled and twirled around the dance floor.

"He's a real rocking horse!" said Greedy Goat.

One morning in the shower, Happy Horse sang,
"I'm H-A-P-P-Y, I'm H-A-P-P-Y!"
as he soaped and bubbled all over.
"That's better," said Happy Horse, as he stepped out of the shower. "A clean horse is a happy horse."

wHOOSH!

Happy Horse stood on the soap, skidded across the floor and slammed nose first into the wall. "oooooOOW!" moaned poor Happy Horse.

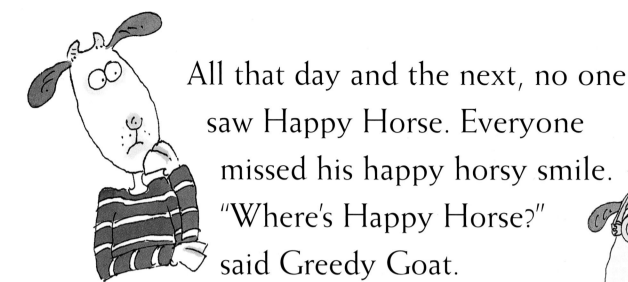

All that day and the next, no one
saw Happy Horse. Everyone
missed his happy horsy smile.
"Where's Happy Horse?"
said Greedy Goat.
"He must be sick,"
said Daft Dog.
"Perhaps he's got a sore throat
and become a little hoarse,"
sniggered Rude Rabbit.

"That's not funny, Rude Rabbit,"
bellowed Mr Cow. "Something
must be wrong."

Then they all went to visit Happy Horse to see what was wrong. They knocked on the door.
Knock! Knock!
But there was no reply. "Yoo Hoo!" shouted Rude Rabbit rudely through the letterbox.
"**Yoo Hoo!**" After a long time the door opened and a very sad face peered out. "What's the matter?" asked Daft Dog. Happy Horse slowly opened his mouth…

"Oh!" Everyone gasped. Right in the middle of Happy Horse's beautiful teeth was a huge gap! "I knocked my toof out and loshht my sshmile," sobbed Happy Horse and a big tear rolled down his cheek and plopped off the end of his nose.

P
L
O
P
!

"Don't cry," said Daft Dog.
"All you need is a dentist."
Happy Horse rolled
his eyes in horror.
"I'm not going to the
dentisht's," he neighed.

Minutes later they all pushed and shoved a very
unwilling Happy Horse into Mr Gnasher's
dental surgery.
"**NO! NO!** I'm sshcared of the dentisht!" cried
Happy Horse as his teeth chattered in fright.
"Don't be a silly Happy Horse," giggled Rude
Rabbit. "Mr Gnasher won't bite you!"

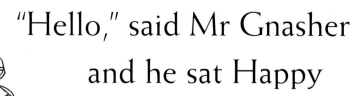

"Hello," said Mr Gnasher and he sat Happy Horse down in his big dentist's chair. Happy Horse was very worried and wanted to bolt off home.

"This won't hurt. Open wide," said Mr Gnasher, as he peered into Happy Horse's big mouth and gently prodded his teeth.

"Aaargh!" said Happy Horse.

"I can fix this," said Mr Gnasher. "Don't worry. Rinse and spit."

"**AAARGH!**" gargled Happy Horse.

Much later Happy Horse galloped out of Mr Gnasher's surgery.

He gave everyone a dazzling smile.
"Wow! That's brilliant," said Daft Dog.
"Look, Mr Gnasher gave me a sticker,
it says *'I love going to the dentist'*,"
said Happy Horse.
"Come back and see
me soon," grinned
Mr Gnasher.
"Yes, I will," said
Happy Horse.
"Thank you
Mr Gnasher."

"Well, that's put the smile back on your face!"
said Rude Rabbit, and Happy Horse
rocked with laughter.